HEY!
THERE'S A GOBLIN Under My Throne!

a KING EDWIN tale
of months and mythical beasts

written & illustrated by
RHETT RANSOM PENNELL

GREENE BARK PRESS
P.O. Box 1108 Bridgeport, Connecticut 06601

To Margaret,
who fills all my months with joy
(and whose startling resemblance to Slugma is only skin deep).

Pennell, Rhett Ransom.
    Hey! There's a goblin under my throne! : (a King
Edwin tale of months & mythical beasts) / written &
illustrated by Rhett Ransom Pennell.
    p. cm.
    SUMMARY: Young King Edwin is forced to defend his
kingdom from monsters sent by Slugma the sorceress. Every
month she sends a different type of monster.
    Audience: Grades 1-3.
    ISBN 1-88085-168-7

    1. Goblins--Juvenile fiction. 2. Months--Juvenile
fiction. 3. Monsters--Juvenile fiction. [1. Goblins--
Fiction. 2. Months--Fiction. 3. Monsters--Fiction.]
I. Title.

PZ7.P384635He 2002   [E]
                QBI02-701997

Warning:

❖

While the monsters
featured in this story
may only have existed in
the minds of imaginative
people who tried to
make sense of the
mysteries of the ancient
world--
THE MONTHS
ARE VERY REAL!!

❖

"Wake up, King Edwin!" whispered the royal knight Sir Gordon. "It's almost midnight. The first day of the new year is about to begin! The people of Yondor are waiting outside to hear your royal blessing."

King Edwin grumbled and snorted as he crawled out of his nice warm bed. Sometimes it was fun to be the King of Yondor…but it was a twenty-four hour a day job!

Edwin stood on the bridge of his castle in the cold of the winter night. "Hello, everybody!" he said. "It's the first day of January. Welcome to a brand new year! May the next twelve months be filled with…*excitement!*"

For a moment the crowd was quiet. Excitement wasn't always a good thing. But they knew the young king meant well, so some of them said, "Hooray for King Edwin!"

Edwin smiled and went back to bed. He had to get some rest while he still could…

…it was going to be a *very* exciting year.

JANUARY

The snow and freezing winter winds of the first month of the year kept most folks inside their homes. That was good -- it meant no one was outside when the Frost Giants came stomping into town.

"Hello, Giants!" yelled King Edwin. "Welcome to my kingdom! Please don't step on anybody while you're here!"

"Oh my!" said the giants. "It's a good thing you said something. You are all so small we didn't even realize you were there."

The Frost Giants headed north with the next snowstorm. They were very careful not to squish anything.

FEBRUARY

The last month of winter was filled with snow and ice…and *goblins!* They came pouring out of the Goblin Forest to the west of Yondor. Soon they were all over the kingdom.

"Hey! There's a goblin under my throne!" yelled King Edwin. "Go back to the Goblin Forest!"

"We can't go back! It's too scary," squeaked the goblin. "We saw Slugma the Sorceress!"

Slugma the Sorceress! This was terrible news.

Slugma was a nasty magician from the dark past of Yondor, when kings were cruel and life was hard.

When Edwin became king, everything changed for the better.

But Slugma liked the way things *used* to be. If she was back, then she was planning to cause trouble.

Edwin commanded his knights to search the forest for Slugma. They didn't find her-- but Sir Gordon and Lady Ada found a note.

"We'll catch her," promised Edwin. "Even if it takes all year."

MARCH

The kingdom slowly grew warmer as the season of spring began. It was time to say goodbye to the snow and hello to the buds of new leaves on the trees.

Usually the melting snow on the mountains trickled down to fill the lakes of Yondor. But now the lakes were nearly empty. Edwin and his knights rode off to find out what was wrong.

"Ooh, I'm sorry," said the ogre stuck in the riverbed, "A strange lady told me I'd find lots of tasty goats if I swam down this stream. I forgot that goats don't swim."

It seemed that Slugma had already begun to make mischief. It took many hours to dig the ogre out and free the water trapped behind him. Everybody got wet.

APRIL

The next month was a mix of sunny days and rainy days--and those rainy days were filled with rumors. Slugma had been spotted stealing a rooster; either she was very hungry…or she was planning to make a basilisk!

A basilisk is a serpent so hideous that anyone who sees it turns to stone. Basilisks only hatch from a rooster's egg (so they're very rare -- since *hens* lay eggs, not roosters). But if anyone could cast a spell to make a rooster lay an egg, it was Slugma.

And sure enough, one rainy day a terrible smell filled the kingdom. "It's a basilisk!" yelled the people of Yondor. "Go to your homes! To see a basilisk is to turn to stone!"

The kingdom was quiet except for the rain... and something hissing and clucking as it slithered though the streets. But then the hissing stopped. The smell was gone! Slowly, the curious people poked their heads out to see what had happened.

There was the basilisk—it had seen it's own reflection in a rain puddle and turned to stone. Now it was just an ugly statue. The sorceress had made a big mistake sending the creature out during a rainstorm.

"We're lucky," said King Edwin. "Slugma is wicked, but she isn't very smart."

MAY

The April showers brought May flowers—which gave a nasty case of hayfever to the manticore that Slugma sent to menace the kingdom. The beast was too busy sneezing to do any harm. "Ah-choo! Ah-choo! Oh dear...*AH-CHOO!!*" he sneezed again and again.

Eventually the manticore became so embarrassed by his runny nose that he ran off to the mountains, tripping over Slugma as he left.

JUNE

The first month of summer was warm and sunny—the perfect month for a wedding. Sir Gordon asked his sweetheart to marry him. She said yes! They were a cute couple, even if he was a royal knight and she was a banshee he had met while on a quest. It was a beautiful ceremony, although some of the guest fairies tended to wail horribly (banshees often wail when something bad is about to happen, but this time they were wailing in happiness for the bride).

Nothing else strange happened in June,
no one could figure out why.

JULY

The next month was hot, hot, hot! The days were long and that big old sun just kept shining down. It was actually a relief when Slugma summoned fire-covered salamanders to attack the castle; it gave Edwin and his knights a reason to use the winter snowballs they had saved in the chilly depths of the castle basement.

"Eek! Those things are *cold!*" shrieked the salamanders as they scurried back to their fiery pits.

AUGUST

The last full month of summer was also the month of Edwin's birthday. The royal party was held in the shade under a thick grove of trees to keep out of the heat. King Edwin got a lot of presents including a new cape, an enchanted shield, and a huge roc that threw stones at everyone while it flew over the kingdom. The knights chased the giant bird away with a barrage of arrows.

The card attached to the roc wasn't signed, but everyone knew who sent *that* present.

SEPTEMBER

As the season of autumn arrived the air began to cool, the leaves on the trees began to turn yellow, and King Edwin's temper turned sour. "I'm tired of Slugma pestering my kingdom," said the king as his knights fought an assortment of golems. "You!" Edwin yelled at the one golem who hadn't been chopped into a pile of clay. "Tell that sorceress to send all her weird creatures to attack us next month. That way we can beat them all at once!"

The king was tiny—but he was *fierce*. The nervous golem ran away to deliver Edwin's message to Slugma.

OCTOBER

And so the next month, as autumn winds howled through the fire-colored trees and gray clouds darkened the sky, Slugma sent a vast army of *things* to storm the castle.

There were bogies, will o'the wisps, sprites, sylphs, kobolds, pixies, virikas, minotaurs, morags, harpies, bunyips, spriggans, spectres, gremlins, tengus, nagas, and many other strange beasts from all the hidden places of the world.

Edwin was ready for them.

In October, there's only one thing to do when monsters come to your home...

...you give them candy.

NOVEMBER

As Autumn neared its end, so did Slugma's supply of monsters. She only had one thing left to use: *herself!*

With a swoop of her hands, Slugma cast a spell that turned the boots of all the knights into heavy stones. They couldn't move! They couldn't help their king!

Slugma stomped to the royal castle. "Edwin!" she yelled. "You've defeated every creature I've sent to chase you away, but you won't defeat *me*. Come out and face me, King Baby!"

Edwin stepped out from his castle. He carried his wooden practice sword (he wasn't old enough for a real sword yet) and the enchanted shield he'd gotten for his birthday. He didn't want to face Slugma alone, but he had to protect his kingdom.

"You are under arrest, Slugma," said the little king as he stood before the sorceress.

Slugma laughed horribly. "Oh, no, no, no! It's *my* turn to live in the castle and *your* turn to hide in the forest," she said. "Or better yet, I'll bring the forest to you! I'll turn you into a King Baby tree!"

Slugma waved her arms and cast a spell, but Edwin was quick and thrust out his enchanted shield. The spell bounced off the shield. It scattered everywhere, sizzling and flashing, and one part hit Slugma right on the nose.

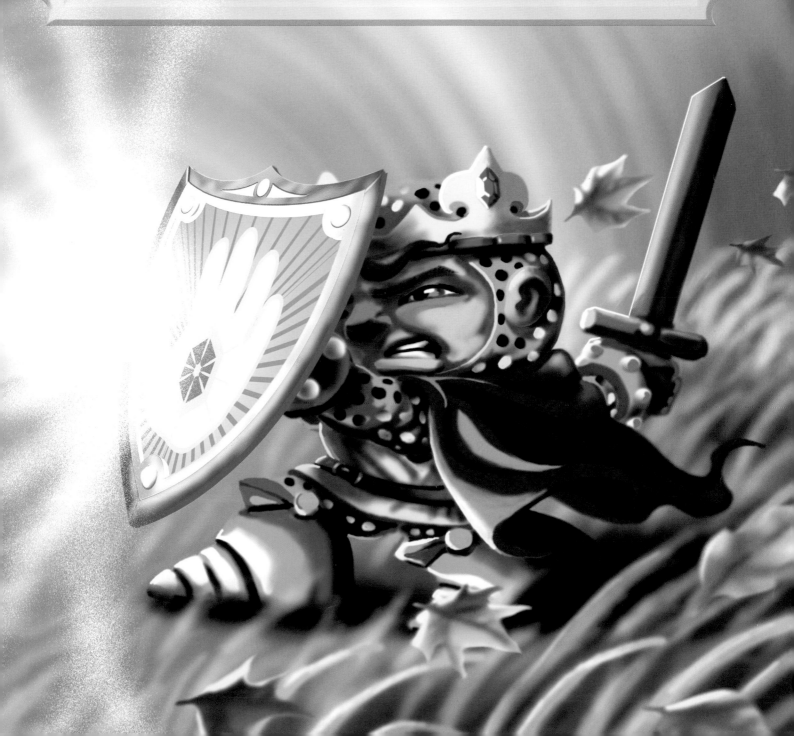

Poof! Slugma was gone—a twisted tree stood in her place. Its branches groaned in the wind, as if to say "Oh, dear."

Oh, how the people of Yondor cheered! King Edwin had defeated Slugma! There would be no more monsters in the kingdom (well, except for the ones that were already there).

DECEMBER

It grew cold and snowy as another winter season rolled into the kingdom, but the people of Yondor were warm in their hearts. The short days and long nights were filled with celebrations and holidays. There were parties to celebrate the end of an exciting year, parties to say goodbye to the goblins as they returned to the Goblin Forest, and parties to honor King Edwin, the best king Yondor ever had.

Even the Slugma Tree was included in the fun.
Sometimes it almost seemed like the tree was smiling.

And so, twelve exciting months had passed and once again King Edwin stood on his bridge at midnight. He was a year older, a few inches taller, and still just as sleepy. The people of Yondor were there to hear his royal blessing, hoping he wasn't going to wish for excitement again.

"Hello, everybody!" said Edwin, "It's the first day of January. Welcome to a brand new year! May the next twelve months be filled with…happiness and chocolate cake!"

The people of Yondor liked this blessing *MUCH* more than the last one. "Hooray for King Edwin!" the entire crowd cheered. "Happy New Year to us all!"